Poppy's Last Chance

Collect all six Arctica Mermaid books

Also look out for the six original Mermaid SOS adventures in Coral Kingdom

Poppy's Last Chance

gillian shields

illustrated by helen turner

BLOOMSBURY
CHILDREN'S
BOOKS

Follow the Arctica

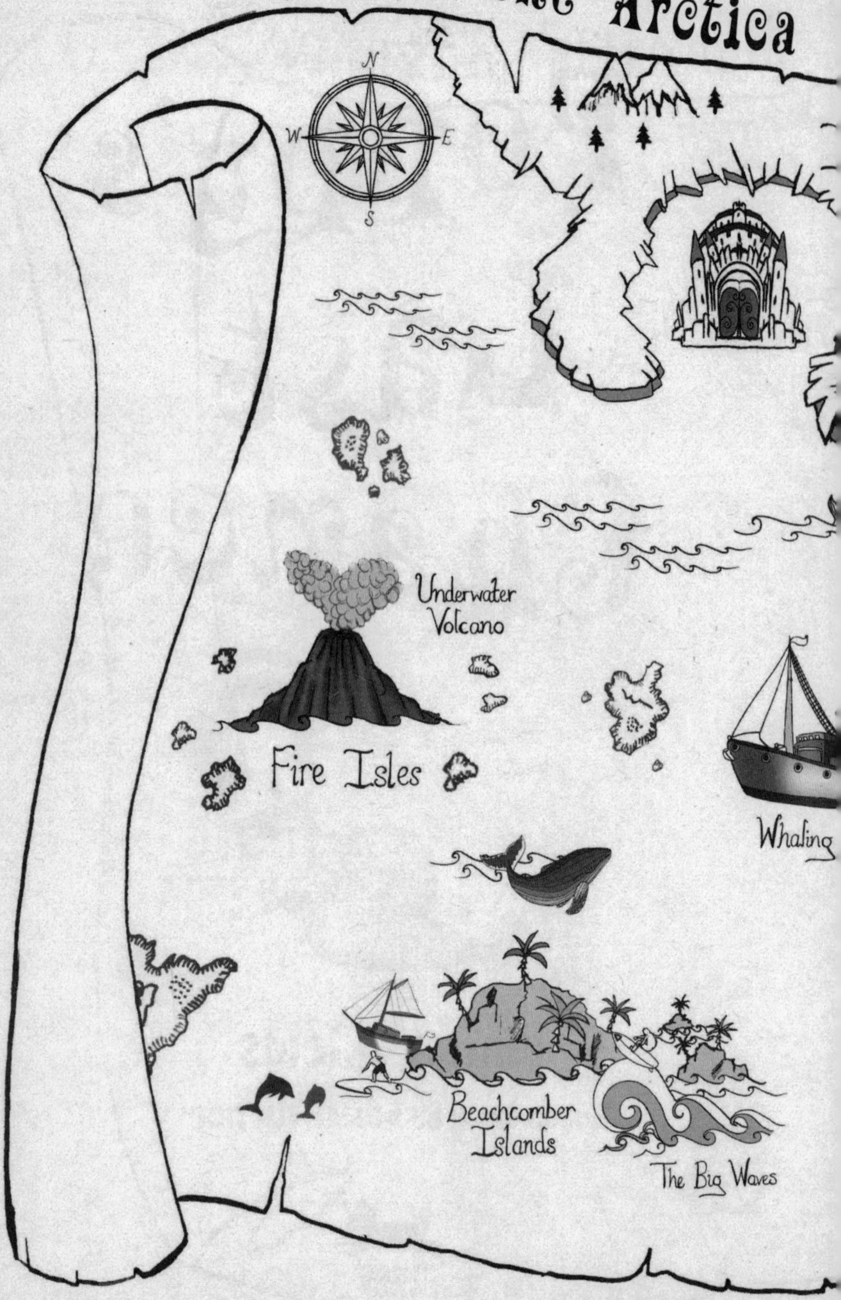

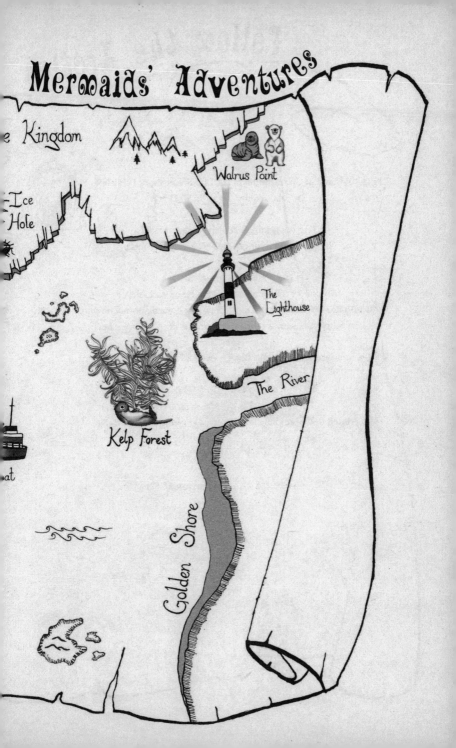

First published in Great Britain in 2007 by Bloomsbury Publishing Plc,
36 Soho Square, London, W1D 3QY

A CIP catalogue record of this book is available from the British Library

ISBN 978 0 7475 8973 0

Printed and bound in Great Britain by Clays Ltd, St Ives Plc

1 3 5 7 9 10 8 6 4 2

www.bloomsbury.com/mermaidSOS

For the children of
Waverley Primary School
— G.S.

To the 'Graphics Girls' from
my happy university days —
Amy, Anna, Emily and Marie
— Love H.T.

Prologue

When the evil mermaid, Mantora, tried
to destroy Coral Kingdom, she was
outwitted by Misty and her young
mermaid friends. Now she is hatching
another terrible plot! This time it is
against Ice Kingdom, the frozen realm
of Princess Arctica.

Mantora has stolen six precious Snow
Diamonds from the underwater Ice
Cavern. Not only that, she has trapped
Princess Arctica and her good Merfolk

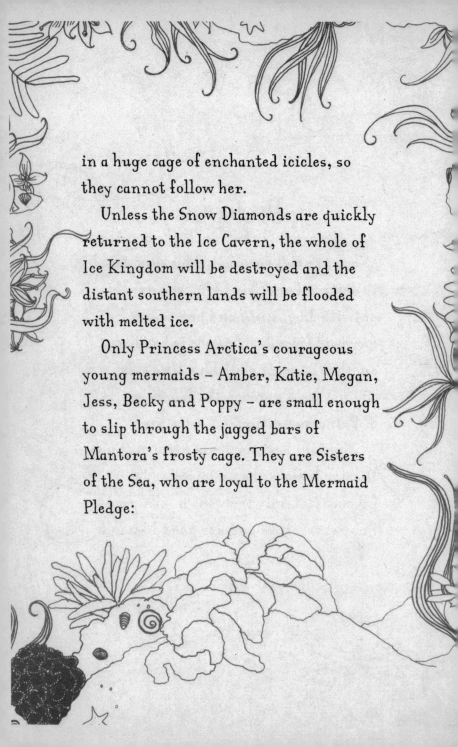

in a huge cage of enchanted icicles, so
they cannot follow her.

Unless the Snow Diamonds are quickly
returned to the Ice Cavern, the whole of
Ice Kingdom will be destroyed and the
distant southern lands will be flooded
with melted ice.

Only Princess Arctica's courageous
young mermaids – Amber, Katie, Megan,
Jess, Becky and Poppy – are small enough
to slip through the jagged bars of
Mantora's frosty cage. They are Sisters
of the Sea, who are loyal to the Mermaid
Pledge:

We promise that we'll take good care
Of all sea creatures everywhere.
We'll never hurt and never break,
We'll always give and never take.
And as we fight Mantora's threat,
This saying we must not forget:
'I'll help you and you'll help me,
For we are Sisters of the Sea!'

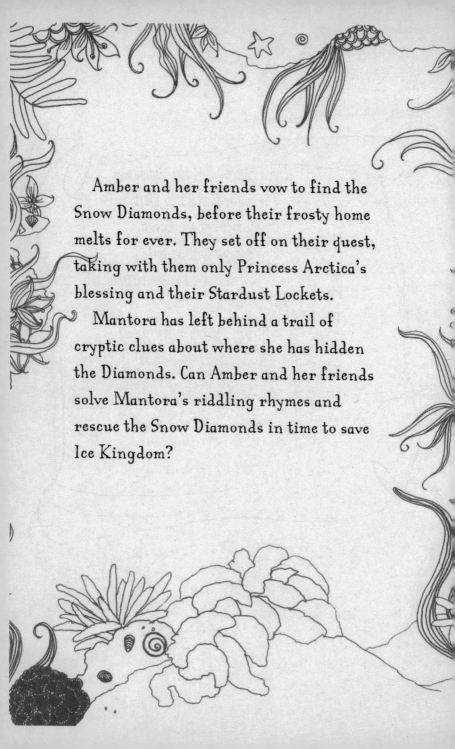

Amber and her friends vow to find the
Snow Diamonds, before their frosty home
melts for ever. They set off on their quest,
taking with them only Princess Arctica's
blessing and their Stardust Lockets.

Mantora has left behind a trail of
cryptic clues about where she has hidden
the Diamonds. Can Amber and her friends
solve Mantora's riddling rhymes and
rescue the Snow Diamonds in time to save
Ice Kingdom?

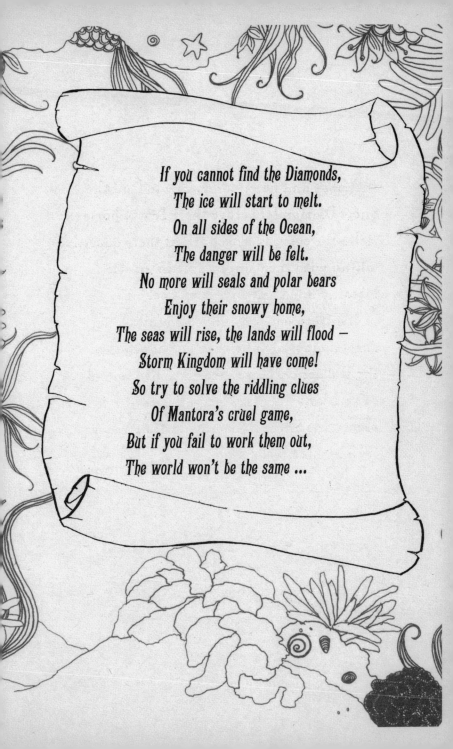

If you cannot find the Diamonds,
The ice will start to melt.
On all sides of the Ocean,
The danger will be felt.
No more will seals and polar bears
Enjoy their snowy home,
The seas will rise, the lands will flood —
Storm Kingdom will have come!
So try to solve the riddling clues
Of Mantora's cruel game,
But if you fail to work them out,
The world won't be the same ...

Poppy

Chapter One

Poppy woke up and moaned faintly. Her head ached and she felt dizzy. She slowly sat up on her sparkly blue tail and looked around the lonely, moonlit cove.

Her mermaid friends – Amber, Katie, Megan, Jess and Becky – were lying asleep on the sand near the waves. Of course! Everything came back to Poppy in a sudden flash. Mantora had been here, and

she had cast a dark spell on the young
mermaids, sending them into an
enchanted sleep. That's what had given
Poppy such a headache.

'Amber! Jess!' Poppy cried anxiously as
she shook her friends. 'Megan! Wake up,
oh, please wake up!'

One by one, the mermaids opened their
eyes, blinking in confusion.

'Oooh, what happened?' they murmured as they sat up and rubbed their sore heads. 'Was Mantora really here? Or was it just a nightmare?'

'Mantora was here all right,' gasped Jess suddenly. 'And this is the proof!'

She held up her arm. A silver bracelet glinted at her wrist. Hanging from the bracelet was a magical Stardust Locket where she had hidden her Snow Diamond. So far the mermaids had found five of the Diamonds which had been stolen by Mantora. They only needed to find one more before racing back to Ice Kingdom with the precious jewels. But Jess was staring at her open Locket in dismay. It was empty!

'Look – my Diamond has gone!' she cried.

Amber, Katie, Megan and Becky

hurriedly checked their own Stardust Lockets. Poppy hadn't got a Diamond yet, because the mermaids had been searching for the last one when Mantora had unexpectedly attacked them.

'My Diamond has disappeared as well,' said Katie, in a worried voice.

'So has mine!' cried Amber.

'And ours too!' added Becky and Megan. 'Wherever can they be?'

'I don't think that's a very difficult mystery to solve,' replied Jess grimly. 'When Mantora put that sleeping spell on us, she must have grabbed the Diamonds from our Lockets.'

'But that means we're right back to square one,' groaned Amber. 'I can hardly believe it, after all our efforts!'

The unhappy mermaids hung their heads in bitter disappointment. They thought about Princess Arctica and their families back home in Ice Kingdom, where they had been trapped by Mantora in a cage of black icicles. The little mermaids had vowed to find the Diamonds, save Ice Kingdom, and free their friends. How could they bear to tell Princess Arctica

that they had failed in their quest?

Poppy felt the most miserable of all. She knew that this terrible situation was really her fault. She blushed as red as her coppery curls, and tears sprang into her eyes.

'I'm sorry,' she wept. 'This is all because of me. Mantora must have heard me bragging that we'd found the first five Diamonds. That gave her the idea to snatch them back!'

'Don't blame yourself, Poppy,' said Becky kindly.

'I should blame myself,' Poppy burst out. 'I've been a nuisance all along. I've been silly and snappy and headstrong. I thought I knew best about everything. But I don't deserve to be called a Sister of the Sea!' She began to sob again.

Amber and the others tried to comfort Poppy, holding her hands and drying her eyes. She began to calm down, and a little voice broke the silence.

'Everyone deserves a second chance.'

The mermaids turned to look at Sammy the Fairy Shrimp, who was perched on Megan's shoulder. A magic sprinkle from her Stardust Locket had given him special powers. Although he was only small, he had

bravely helped the mermaids on their quest.

'You're right, Sammy,' said Megan.
'Don't worry, Poppy, we'll give you
another chance to prove yourself.'

'How?' sniffed Poppy, as she rubbed her
tear-stained eyes.

'By not letting Mantora get away with
this,' exclaimed Jess. 'It's no good sitting
around crying. We've simply got to get
those five Diamonds back before it's too
late – and find the last one!'

The others looked up hopefully. Even
Poppy managed a watery smile.

'All right,' she promised. 'I'll find the
Diamonds somehow. It will be my last
chance to prove to you – and to Princess
Arctica – that I really am a true Sister of
the Sea.' She took a deep breath. 'Now,

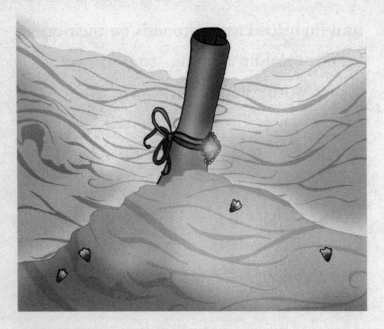

where shall we start?'

'Let's see if Mantora has left any clues behind,' suggested Katie. The mermaids glanced around the deserted beach. Poppy suddenly noticed something that was half-buried in the sand. It was a roll of black parchment, sealed with a red jewel.

'This must be a message from Mantora,'

said Poppy, tearing it open. 'Perhaps it is
one final riddle for us to solve. Listen!

'The end is near,

Of this great race,

And what you fear

Will soon take place.

Under the waves

The fire will glow,

As in the secret caves,

Mantora will go.

The Diamonds rare,

Your pride and joy,

And Ice Kingdom fair –

I will destroy!

You will never find me, or the Diamonds now.

P.S. Your quest is over.

There is nothing left for you to do, but despair...'

27

'That's what you think, Mantora,' said Poppy, her eyes shining with determination. 'We're not going to give up so easily.'

'But how can there be fire under the water?' wondered Megan. 'That's impossible!'

The others looked bewildered, too. They couldn't imagine how such a strange thing could exist.

'And where are the secret caves?' added
Amber.

'Well, wherever they are, we have to get
there quickly,' said Jess practically, 'before
Mantora really does destroy the Diamonds.'

'Why don't we ask Monty?' said Becky.
'His folk swim in these parts on their
long journeys every year.
He might be able to
help us.'

'Good idea!'
replied Poppy
gratefully. 'Come
on, let's
hurry.'

The friends slipped into the sea and dived swiftly under the waves. The morning sun was just beginning to peep over the horizon. With a ripple of their glistening tails, the mermaids swam to where Monty the whale was waiting for them in the deep waters of the bay.

'Monty!' the mermaids called. 'We have to find the secret caves…and the underwater fire…we must hurry…'

'Whoa, steady,' rumbled the friendly humpback whale. 'The underwater fire? We whales have heard the legend of the Forbidden Mountain, where they say a great fire burns under the water. But I thought it was just a story. None of my folk have ever seen it.'

'But we have to find it,' pleaded Poppy.

'The clue says it's important.'

'There's only one thing to do, then,' replied Monty. 'We must ask the creatures who live in these waters if there really is such a place as the Forbidden Mountain. We must call a Council of the Sea!'

Chapter Two

Poppy and her friends looked at one
another with solemn faces. A Council of
the Sea was a special meeting that was
only called in the most serious
emergencies. The young mermaids had
never been to one before.

'How do we tell everyone about it?'
asked Poppy.

'Like this!' said Monty. 'Join in with me,

everyone.' He
lifted his head
and gave a
long, haunting
cry which
echoed through
the waves. 'In
the name of
Queen Neptuna
and her cousin
Princess

Arctica, we summon all loyal folk to a
Council of the Sea!'

Then the mermaids swam around
Monty, weaving in and out like bright
ribbons round a maypole. As they swam,
Katie played her Mermaid Harp and the
friends sang an urgent song:

33

'*Shark and Turtle,*
Dolphin, Fish,
Listen to our
Dearest wish;
If you care
About the sea,
Come to me,
Oh, come to me!
Loyal friends
If you are near,
We need you now,
We need you here!'

Poppy paused for breath as a strange parade of sea creatures swam through the clear water. There were curious dolphins, green turtles, noisy seals, and all sorts of multi-coloured fish. There was even a

good-tempered hammerhead shark, with a
family of little starfish perched on his broad
head. It seemed that every creature in the
sea had answered the mermaids' call.

'Greetings!' the creatures cried out as
they circled the mermaids under the water.
'What's happening? Why
have you summoned us?'

'We need
your help,'
explained
Poppy. 'The
Ocean is in
great danger.'

'Danger!'
squealed a
baby starfish,
nearly falling

off the shark's head in fright. 'That sounds…dangerous!'

Some of the other creatures giggled.

'Shhh,' said the mother starfish to her baby, glaring round crossly at the others. 'And "Shhh!" to the rest of you!'

Everyone settled down again to listen to Poppy.

'We really do have a serious problem,' she began. 'That's why we have called you to this Council.'

'There can't be a Council without the Eagles,' objected an old turtle. 'They are the wisest creatures round here. The Eagles will give you good advice.'

'The Eagles?' said Poppy, in a puzzled voice. 'Do you mean the fierce birds who live in the Overwater world?' Surely there

37

couldn't be *eagles* under the sea, she thought, as well as fire? It all seemed topsy-turvy and upside down...

'No!' replied the turtle. 'We mean the great Eagle Rays who patrol our waters. And here they are!'

Everyone turned and watched as six unusual creatures with slim, flat bodies glided towards them. They swam like fish, yet had graceful flapping wings like birds. The Eagle Rays had arrived!

'We have come to the Council, oh Sisters of the Sea,' said the leader. 'My name is Rakesh. What is your desire?'

Poppy suddenly felt shy in front of the stately Eagle Rays.

'P-please, sir,' she stammered. 'We need to find the secret caves that lead to the

Forbidden Mountain – that is, if it really exists.'

The dolphins, turtles and fish gasped in surprise. Even Rakesh looked puzzled.

'You speak boldly of the Forbidden

Mountain,' he frowned. 'It is not for all
folk to know of such things. And besides,
why would six little mermaids need to
follow that path of danger?'

'Because Mantora is taking the Snow
Diamonds there, and she's going to destroy
them,' exclaimed Poppy. 'If she does, Ice

Kingdom will melt. Your seas here will rise, the lands will be flooded and the whole world will become too warm. Everyone's home is in danger – and it's all my fault,' she added miserably. 'So, if you do know anything about the mountain, please, *please* give me a chance to put my mistakes right.'

Rakesh seemed impressed by the young mermaid's passionate words.

'I can tell that you have spoken honestly,' he said gravely. 'To tell the truth is one of the simplest deeds, yet it can also be the hardest.' The leader of the Eagle Rays glanced round slowly. 'I will also speak the truth. The Mountain does indeed exist.'

The mermaids looked excited. 'Can you

please tell us where it is?' asked Jess
eagerly.

'It is hidden in the deep sea below the
Fire Isles, where we sometimes roam in our
search for secret places to bring up our
young,' replied Rakesh. 'We can take you
there, if it will help your mission. But
beware! It is risky to disturb the
Mountain's sleeping power.'

Some of the creatures looked rather frightened. The mother starfish caught hold of one of her baby's five arms and dragged him away, muttering, 'Sorry! Just remembered that we have to…er…um…go home!' A few others darted away after them. But the mermaids looked determined.

'We are willing to face any danger to fulfil our quest,' said Amber quietly. The other mermaids nodded in agreement, and Monty rumbled, 'Hrrumph! And I will come with them, to the ends of the Ocean.'

'And so will I!' squeaked little Sammy.

'Then let us go at once,' said Rakesh. 'Mermaids, you can ride with Monty. And now, let us speed on our way.'

Swooping through the clear water, the

Eagle Rays streamed ahead. Monty followed behind, bearing Poppy and her friends on his back. The dolphins, seals and turtles let out a cheer as the mermaids set off once more on the Whale Express. The courageous young Sisters of the Sea were heading for the Forbidden Mountain, and for danger…

Chapter Three

Poppy peered over the broad curve of
Monty's back with wide, wondering eyes.
They had been travelling for a long time,
and now they were following the Eagle
Rays into deep water — deeper than the
mermaids had ever been before. It was
dark and murky. Odd-looking fish with
big, staring eyes hovered in the nooks and
crannies of the sea bed.

'Where are we, Rakesh?' Poppy called out nervously. The leader of the Eagle Rays came to a gliding halt.

'We are near the underwater roots of the Fire Isles,' he replied. 'We have done the easy part of our journey. But the way to the secret caves and the Mountain lies below, in these dark waters. Anyone who wishes to turn back must do so now!'

No one spoke. A silent ripple of determination ran through the mermaids, though Poppy felt that everyone must be able to hear her heart thumping wildly.

'We do not wish to turn back,' she forced herself to say. 'Please show us the way.'

'Very well,' said Rakesh, 'but be on your guard. Many strange creatures live in these deeps, and they are not all friendly.'

Very quietly, Monty and the Rays floated forward in the gloomy water. There was not very much light coming from above, but clumps of special seaweed grew here and there, which gave off a ghostly green glow. Poppy's spine prickled with goose bumps.

SNAP! CRASH! CRUNCH!

A bright light flashed in front of the mermaids' eyes and the snapping of jaws made them all jump. Megan let out a little shriek. An ugly, scary face had suddenly darted into view. It was a mean-looking anglerfish, with a hunting lure hanging from his drooping antenna. He snapped his fierce jaws together again.

'Ooooh!' said Megan, hiding her face in her hands. 'He's trying to get me!'

Poppy looked up quickly. 'It's not you he wants,' she exclaimed. 'It's Sammy!'

The horrid fish was darting after the tiny Fairy Shrimp, trying to catch him for a tasty snack. Sammy was zig-zagging to and fro in a panic, hiding behind each of the mermaids in turn.

'Sammy! Sammy!' shouted Megan, flapping her hands at the anglerfish to try to frighten him off. 'Stay out of his way!'

Without having time to think, Amber pulled open the little bag that Ana the Inuit girl had given her.

'Here Sammy,' she urged. 'Swim in here!'

The Fairy Shrimp shot through the water and landed in the bag, just as the anglerfish was trying to catch him with its

49

terrible teeth. Amber quickly tied the neck
of the bag so that the anglerfish couldn't
see Sammy any more.

'Shoo! Go away!' cried the mermaids.

Finally, the anglerfish gave up the chase
and swam away, with a last dreadful glare
at the young friends. They shivered with
relief, but Rakesh had been right – this
really was a dangerous part of the sea.

'Oh, Sammy, thank goodness you're
safe,' sighed Megan, as Amber undid the

bag once more. Sammy peeped out, looking very scared.

'You must be more careful down here, Sammy,' said Katie. 'That was scary!'

'We must all be careful,' called Rakesh. 'The entrance to the secret caves lies ahead.'

A tall ring of rocks rose up in front of the mermaids, as high as they could see. The rocks were riddled with holes like a honeycomb. A series of caves and caverns led into the heart of the rocks, where

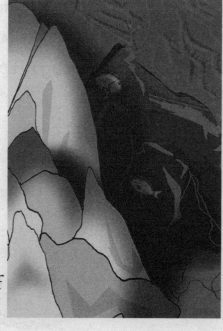

the Forbidden Mountain was hidden.

'We must swim through those caves and tunnels, mermaids, to reach the Mountain at the centre,' said Rakesh.

'Oh, but…' said Jess '…those holes, and the caves…they're much too small for Monty to swim through!'

Everyone looked at the mighty whale in concern. It was true, he would never be able to wriggle through the narrow openings.

'Then you have a choice, mermaids,' Rakesh replied. 'Either to leave your whale friend at the entrance to the caves, or to abandon your quest.'

'But we can't leave Monty,' gasped Jess. She was firm friends with their loyal companion.

'And we can't give up now,' said Poppy, with a concerned expression.

'Don't worry, mermaids,' said Monty. 'I'll go back up to the surface for some air and wait for you there. But be careful.'

Jess flung her arms round his nose and kissed him.

'We'll see you soon, Monty,' she cried, in a shaky voice. 'After we have solved the final clue!'

Monty began to glide away through the

dreary waters, up towards the sunlight.
Then Rakesh called the mermaids to
attention.

'We are now entering the secret places,'
he said. 'You may ride on our backs. It
will be quicker and safer.'

Poppy and her friends felt very proud,
perched on the backs of the Eagle Rays. It
really felt like flying through the water.
With a swirl of bubbles, they twisted and
turned through the rocky tunnels. When
they emerged on the other side, the
Forbidden Mountain rose in gloomy
splendour from the sea bed. Cloudy fumes
and jets of hot water spouted from its
cone-shaped head. In the Mountain's deep
heart, red molten lava glowed like a living
jewel.

'Why, it's a volcano!' stuttered Amber.

'An *underwater* volcano,' added Becky, in an awestruck voice. 'That's amazing.'

'It's just how the clue said it would be,' exclaimed Megan. '"*Under the waves the fire will glow*".'

'Don't forget what the next part said,' murmured Katie apprehensively. '"*As in the secret caves, Mantora will go*".'

'And look over there, everyone,' said Jess.

The mermaids gazed up at where she was pointing, high on the side of the volcano. Near to its smoking crown, a glistening figure was hovering in the murky sea.

'It's Mantora!' gasped Poppy.

Chapter Four

Poppy leaned forward and whispered
urgently to Rakesh, 'We must go after
Mantora – and let's hope that she still has
the Diamonds.'

The Eagle Rays flapped their huge
wings and soared up through the cloudy
water.

'*Mermaid SOS!*' cried the brave young
friends, as they rode on the great Rays,

their hair streaming out behind them. Higher and higher they went, until the mermaids were on a level with their great enemy. But Mantora was not alone. She was surrounded by a gang of Goblin Sharks, with flabby skin and thrusting snouts.

Mantora swished her bronze tail and turned to stare at the little mermaids. In one hand she held her netted spear. In the other, she clutched all six of the radiant Snow Diamonds. In this murky place, they shone even more brilliantly than before. Their sparkling rays of pure light were like a message of hope.

The fumes from the volcano made Poppy want to choke and sneeze, and she could feel her cheeks burning. But she knew this was her only chance to rescue the Diamonds. She called out, 'In the name of Queen Neptuna, I order you to give me the Snow Diamonds. They are not yours, Mantora. They belong to all the free folk of the Ocean. Give them back!'

'You think you can order *me*, the Queen of Storm and Darkness?' screeched Mantora. 'How dare you! I will do what I please with these stupid baubles. I have

come here to throw them into the volcano's
deep fire. That will destroy them for ever –
and your feeble Ice Kingdom! Ha, ha, ha!'

Mantora's Goblin Sharks grinned,
flashing their rows of spiked teeth, as she
continued, 'After that, the Mountain will
destroy you! Don't you know it is
forbidden for small fry like you to come
into its secret places?'

She lifted her hand, getting ready to cast
the Diamonds into the hot open mouth of
the volcano.

'STOP!' said a deep voice. It was Rakesh.
'And don't you know, Mantora – Queen of
Nothing and Nowhere – that it is forbidden
to come here with evil purposes?'

For a moment a look of doubt flashed
across Mantora's face.

'The Mountain is fierce, but not evil,' Rakesh continued. 'It too is part of Mother Nature's great world. If you cast the precious Diamonds into the fire, you will disturb its powers. Then it is you who will be destroyed. Do as this young mermaid says – give them back!'

'If you do not give the Diamonds willingly, we will take them,' said Poppy, in a clear voice.

Instantly, Mantora spat out her reply. 'I

am guarded by my sharks and armed with my spear,' she sneered. 'You have nothing on your side but these flapping Rays and an idiotic shrimp! How do you imagine that you would ever get the Diamonds from me?'

'Like this!' cried the brave young mermaids.

They held up their Stardust Lockets, and sang together:

'Light of the Star
Shine under the Sea,
Give us our wish,
Set the Diamonds free!'

Blinding ribbons of light shot out from the Lockets and stung the Goblin Sharks, who yelped and darted away. Then the magical light wound itself like silver ropes around Mantora, who was trying to slash her way free with her spear. But it was too late. She was trapped in a glittering cage of woven light.

'Let me out! Let me…aaaagh!'

Mantora screamed as the Snow Diamonds flew from her hand, spinning through the dark water like bright stars. One by one, they settled into the six Stardust Lockets, safe once more. Mantora groaned, but the mermaids cheered.

'Hooray!' they cried. 'Oh, well done, Poppy. You were brilliant.'

'Thank you,' she smiled. 'We made a great team, didn't we? And thank you,

Rakesh. We couldn't have done it without you.'

'My brothers and I were happy to help you,' said the noble Eagle Ray. 'Princess Arctica will be proud of you.'

Princess Arctica! Now that the mermaids had all six Snow Diamonds at last, their thoughts turned to home.

'What if Ice Kingdom has already stared to melt?' worried Katie. 'The Snow Diamonds have been missing from their casket in the Ice Cavern for several days now.

I do hope we won't be too late.'

'And I hope Princess Arctica and our families are all right, stuck like prisoners in that horrible cage of icicles,' murmured Amber.

'Talking of prisoners,' said Jess, 'what are we going to do with Mantora?'

They glanced over to where Mantora was still writing at the volcano's edge, caught in the magical chains of light. The Mountain rumbled, and hot fumes bubbled up from its depths. Mantora struggled desperately to get away.

Poppy shrugged. 'It's not for us to decide. We must go home now.'

'Don't…leave…me…here!' whined Mantora, between clenched teeth. 'Please…I've changed my mind…I want to help you…'

'Don't trust her, whispered Rakesh. 'Go now! The magical light will not hold her for ever. We will guard her whilst you swim up to the surface and find Monty again. Hurry back to Ice Kingdom with the Diamonds. Or it might be too late when you get there!'

The mermaids streamed upwards, away from the smouldering Mountain, followed by Mantora's enraged shrieks. The last desperate race for Ice Kingdom had begun.

Chapter Five

Monty was surging through the clear green water. The friends had left the Fire Isles behind many hours ago, and were heading straight for Ice Kingdom. The last rays of sunset glowed crimson as they sped along.

Poppy clung to Monty's back and stared at the horizon. She was trying to catch a glimpse of the familiar icebergs and snowy plains of their northern home. But at that moment, the mermaids heard a sound that they dreaded.

'Aaaark! Uuuuurk!' The harsh cries were coming from overhead.

'Storm Gulls!' shouted Jess. 'And they're heading this way. Mantora must have sent them somehow.'

'Dive from my back and swim for home as fast as you can, Mermaids,' boomed Monty. 'I'll deal with these carrion crows. We will meet again in Ice Kingdom. Now go!'

Instantly, the mermaids slipped from Monty and plunged into the cool waves. Poppy caught a glimpse of Monty lifting his huge tail out of the water, ready to bat the black Gulls out of his way. Then she saw no more as she sank deep under the water, swimming next to her friends.

Without speaking, they raced along for what seemed like miles and miles. They were using every muscle, every breath and every drop of strength to get nearer to Ice Kingdom.

'I...c-can't...go...any...further,' Becky finally gasped. 'Where are we?'

'Let's risk going to the surface to look,' answered Jess. 'I'm sure Monty dealt with those Storm Gulls, so it should be safe.'

As Poppy and her friends cautiously peeped over the waves, a dazzling sight met their eyes. All around them, the vast snowy realm of Ice Kingdom gleamed and shone in the moonlight. The North Star blazed above the mermaids, welcoming them home.

'We've made it!' cried the brave young

friends, hugging one another happily.

'But look,' said Poppy, when they had calmed down. 'What's happening to the icebergs?'

Large splashy drops of water, like tears, were running down the sides of the icebergs. Little trickling streams made their way across the flat plains of ice. The constant sound of *drip, drip, plink, plink,* echoed through the night air.

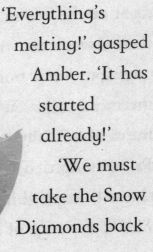

'Everything's melting!' gasped Amber. 'It has started already!'

'We must take the Snow Diamonds back

to Princess Arctica
straight away,'
said Katie.
'Did you say
Princess Arctica?' said a
mournful voice. The
mermaids twirled round and saw a pale
white face gleaming in the water.

'Benjy!' they shouted. It was the baby
beluga whale they had rescued
right at the beginning of
their adventures. A hundred
questions burst from the
mermaids' lips. 'What's
happening? Where is
Princess Arctica? Is
she still trapped in
Mantora's cage of icicles?'

'She is,' said Benjy, 'and she needs
your help. Ana and I have taken turns to
watch for you by day and night. You must
swim to the Palace at once – Princess
Arctica is in an enchanted sleep and
cannot wake up!'

The mermaids looked at one another in
horror. This was even worse than they had
feared. Ice Kingdom was beginning to
melt – and now there was this dreadful
news about Princess Arctica. There was
not a moment to lose.

'Thank you, Benjy,' said Poppy. 'This
way, everyone!'

She darted back under the waves,
seeking the entrance to the underwater Ice
Palace. Soon, the mermaids were
swimming through its wide open gates.

There was a deathly hush over the home of the Merfolk. Gliding down the empty corridors, Poppy and her friends arrived at the Great Chamber. This was where they had last seen Princess Arctica and their families. As they swam into the Chamber, they heard the soft sound of weeping.

The huge cage of enchanted black icicles still stood in the middle of the Chamber, which was hollowed out of glistening rock. The weary Merfolk were huddled in the cage, gathered sadly next to Princess Arctica. She lay in a deep sleep. Her fair hair tumbled around her and her skin was as white as snow.

Poppy swooped forward with a ripple of her tail. 'We're back,' she cried. 'And we've brought the Snow Diamonds!'

The Merfolk looked up in astonishment. They were torn between joy at the sight of the young mermaids, and sorrow at the fate of their Princess. There were tears and smiles on every face.

'We will release you from this cage, then help the Princess,' promised Amber.

For the last time, the Mermaids held up their Stardust Lockets and sang gladly:

'Freedom, sweet freedom,
We bring you today,
Down with these cages –
All barriers away!
The power of the Diamonds
In Lockets so bright
Releases our Merfolk,
And puts all to right!'

A rainbow of glitter streamed from each Stardust Locket and wound round the bars of the cage. In an instant, the icicles crumbled away, the cage disappeared and the Merfolk were free. Poppy and her friends flung themselves into the arms of their families. They were so happy to be near their loved ones again.

But this was not yet the time for rejoicing. The Diamonds had to be returned to their casket in the secret Ice Cavern, and Princess Arctica still lay asleep.

'What happened to the Princess?' asked Poppy. 'She looks so deathly pale.'

'It was just after you set off to find the

Diamonds,' answered a wise old merman with a long beard. 'Mantora came swooping back in here, brandishing her spear. She muttered some words, there was a flash of green light and she vanished. Then Princess Arctica fell asleep, and we can't wake her!'

The mermaids looked sorrowfully at Princess Arctica. Perhaps the Stardust Lockets would be able to help her? But before they could do or say anything, Sammy suddenly wriggled out of Megan's pocket and hovered in the water near the Princess's lovely face. Then he plunged under a thick strand of her shining hair that lay across her neck.

'Sammy!' cried Megan. 'Whatever are you doing?'

But the little Fairy Shrimp
stubbornly tugged at something
hidden by the Princess's shining
curls.

'Just...trying...to...
pull...this...out...'
Sammy puffed. Then
he fell backwards,
clutching a black
feather. It was from a
Storm Gull and had been
tangled in Princess Arctica's shining hair.

'Oh dear, I feel...so...sleepy,' murmured
the tiny shrimp. Then Sammy promptly
fell asleep!

'This magical feather must have been
why Princess Arctica couldn't wake up,'
said Poppy in amazement. 'Mantora must

have hidden it in her hair without anyone noticing. And now that Sammy has touched the feather, he's asleep too!'

Amber quickly took a silk handkerchief from the soft bag which Ana had given her. Covering her fingers with the handkerchief, Amber picked up the enchanted feather without touching it, wrapped it in the silky material and thrust it out of sight in the bag. As soon as she did so, Sammy woke up, looking rather surprised.

'That just shows that you can't trust a Storm Gull – not even their feathers!' he squeaked.

'And it shows that you don't have to be big to be a hero,' said Princess Arctica, in a sweet, rippling voice. She had opened her eyes and was sitting up on her silver tail. The blue sapphires in her jewelled belt sparkled, and her cheeks bloomed like roses. The little mermaids and the good Merfolk cheered wildly to see her restored to them.

'How can I ever thank you, my faithful little friend?' she said to Sammy, who blushed a deep pink. 'And you too, my brave young mermaids?'

'It doesn't matter about being thanked,' stammered Poppy. 'We just want to put the Snow Diamonds safely in their casket, so that Ice Kingdom won't melt. The tips of the icebergs are already dripping into the sea.'

'Then follow me, dear friends,' said Princess Arctica. She gracefully uncoiled

her tail and swam across the chamber.
'Let's go to the Ice Cavern!'

Chapter Six

Poppy, Amber, Katie, Megan, Jess, Becky
and Sammy swam after the Princess,
through the twisting underwater passages
that led to the Ice Cavern. They pushed
open the carved door and slipped into the
secret treasure store. The wonderful statues
were still there: the Fish, the Dolphin, the
Sea Bird, the flowery Anemone, the Star
and the great Heart. The statues guarded

the glittering casket on its pillar of ice, where the Snow Diamonds belonged.

'Your brave hearts helped you to complete your task,' said Princess Arctica, 'as well as your love for the sea and all its

creatures.' As she gazed at each one of the mermaids with her piercing blue eyes, the Princess seemed to know everything that had happened to them. 'Return the Snow Diamonds to the heart of our kingdom, and rejoice.'

Amber, Katie, Megan, Jess and Becky carefully opened their Stardust Lockets and placed their Diamonds in the glittering casket. As they did so, the cavern glowed with swirling colours – red, blue, pink, green

and yellow. Last of all, Poppy swam up to put her Diamond into the sparkling chest.

'Well done, Poppy,' said Princess Arctica, with a smile. 'You took your chance and proved your worth. You are a true Sister of the Sea!'

But just as Poppy was about to let the Snow Diamond slip from her hand into the casket, there was a commotion from behind the pillar of ice. A cloud of dust blew up from the floor of the Cavern like a tornado, and the light grew dim.

Princess Arctica and the little mermaids gasped. There was a swirl of a dark cloak and the swish of a tarnished tail, and Mantora swam out from behind the pillar. She snatched Poppy's hand, curling her bony fingers around the last Snow Diamond.

'Did you really think you could keep me trapped at the Mountain?' she snarled. 'My power is much greater than that!'

'But not as great as mine,' called a rich, musical voice. Poppy looked up in amazement. A beautiful mermaid with a dazzling gold tail had swum into the underwater cavern. She was wearing a glimmering Crystal like a crown, and she was surrounded by a band of lordly Merfolk. Poppy and her friends knew at once who she was.

'Queen Neptuna!' they cried.

'Yes,' said the Queen. 'We have answered your messages for help at last, my dear Arctica. And help is at hand!'

The Queen held up a Crystal sceptre which filled the Cavern with brilliant light. Mantora's spear was shattered into a thousand pieces. The wicked mermaid let go of Poppy's hand with a cry. Mantora's tail curled limply underneath her and she sank grovelling to the floor.

'Mantora, my sister,' sighed Queen Neptuna, 'I banish you from the realm of Princess Arctica for a year and a day. The only way you can be released from this punishment is if you make amends for your selfishness. Do you choose to stay and work for the good of Ice Kingdom, or will you go your own dark way?'

'I choose banishment,' screeched Mantora, her face twisted with jealousy and hate. 'But one day, I'll get my revenge!' She flicked her tail and slithered up from the floor, then swam away as quickly as she could. A faint cry of '*Rev-e-n-g-e....*' echoed after her, and she was gone.

For a moment, Queen Neptuna looked sad. But then she looked at Poppy and her friends with a gracious smile. 'Come,' she said. 'Let us put these bad memories behind us. I shall seal Ice Kingdom with my Mermaid Magic, so that Mantora cannot return in a hurry. But first, Poppy, you have a task to complete.'

With a trembling hand, Poppy held out the last Snow Diamond and placed it in the casket. The statues glowed with glorious colours, the casket shut itself with a snap, and the Snow Diamonds were finally safe at last.

'Hooray!' cried the mermaids.

'Yippee!' squealed Sammy, turning a somersault in the water and making everyone laugh.

'Well done, my brave young mermaids,' smiled Princess Arctica. 'And you must all keep the Stardust Lockets in memory of your great quest to save Ice Kingdom.'

'Oh, thank you, Princess,' said Poppy

eagerly. 'And can we go and see if the icebergs have frozen again, now that the Diamonds are back in the Ice Cavern?'

'But what about seeing our parents first?' asked Megan. 'They'll be longing to talk to us properly.'

'Princess Arctica and I will see your families and the rest of the Merfolk, and tell them of your heroic adventures,' said Queen Neptuna. 'Later, we will have a Royal Feast and there will be time for glad reunions. But first, swim up to the Overwater world. You might find someone else there who is also longing to see you.'

Bursting with curiosity, Poppy and her friends quickly swam out of the Ice Cavern. Soon, the mermaids were floating in the cool waves, near the frosty ice edge.

The stars had faded, and the morning sun was beginning to climb in the sky. A high plume of spray shot into the air over by the horizon.

'That's Monty,' cried Jess joyfully.

'And look over there,' smiled Becky. 'It's Ana!'

The little Inuit girl was hurrying down to the edge of the ice. She flung herself down and hung over the water excitedly.

'You're back,' she panted. 'I'm so happy to see you. And my father says the melting ice has frozen again! So you must have found the other Snow Diamonds and brought them home.'

'Yes, we did,' said Poppy, with a grin at her friends. 'It was quite an adventure.'

'And we brought something for you,

too,' remembered Katie.

Amber opened the little bag that Ana had lent them at the start of their quest and took out a delicate Mermaid Comb, set with gleaming green gems.

'Oh, it's so pretty,' exclaimed Ana. 'Thank you so much.'

'Maya, the island girl, sends this to you with her love and greetings,' said Becky. 'You are both friends of the Merfolk.'

'Do you remember that we told Maya that anyone who took the Mermaid Pledge became our sister?' asked Megan. 'Would you like to do that, Ana? You have helped us in so many ways.'

'And if the Mermaids and the Children of the world work together,' added Poppy hopefully, 'perhaps we can beat Mantora for good, and save our beautiful seas for ever.'

Ana and the mermaids turned to look at the sun coming up over the bright sea. It was a new day, and a new start. Mantora was banished and Ice Kingdom was safe. How good that felt! The friends laughed and held hands, their clear voices ringing out like bells:

'I'll help you and you'll help me,
For we are Sisters of the Sea!'

THE END

. . . For now!

Arctica Mermaid Sisters of the Sea

Amber has golden curls and a gleaming lilac tail. She looks after her friends, and is a good leader.

Katie enjoys playing her Mermaid Harp. She has a long plait over her shoulder and a sparkly lemon-coloured tail.

Megan has sweet wavy hair and a spangled pink and white tail. She is never far from her pet Fairy Shrimp, Sammy.

Jess is bold and brave, with dark curls and a dazzling turquoise tail. She is friends with Monty, the humpback whale.

Becky loves the beauty of the sea. Her hair is decorated with flowers, and her tail is a pretty peach colour.

Poppy has coppery curls, a bright blue tail, and bags of confidence, but her impatience can land her in trouble.